T3-BEA-048

Richard Scarry's
Smokey
the Fireman

A Golden Book • New York

Western Publishing Company, Inc., Racine, Wisconsin 53404

Smokey,
the Best Fire Fighter Ever

Smokey was a fire fighter.
He loved to put out fires.
One day Smokey had
nothing to do.
So he went to sleep.

Down the street a voice cried,
"Help! Help! My house is
full of smoke!"
It was Katie Kitty.

The fire bell began to ring!
Wake up, Smokey!

Smokey jumped up.
He put on his hat.
He put on his boots.
He put on his raincoat.
He slid down the pole.
He jumped into his fire engine.

Clang! Clang! went the bell.
Officer Bob stopped the cars.
Hurry, Smokey!

Oh, no! A pie truck was
in the way.
Pies went flying.
The pieman went flying, too.

They all landed in
Smokey's fire engine!
But Smokey kept on going.
Katie Kitty needed his help.

Smokey hurried up the ladder.
He saved Katie Kitty.
"Oh, thank you, Smokey!"
said Katie.

Then Smokey turned his hose
on the fire.
SWOOOSH!
The fire was out.

Smokey turned his hose
on his fire engine.
SWOOOSH!
His fire engine was red again.

Smokey turned his hose
on the pieman.
SWOOOSH!
The pieman was clean again.

Then everyone went inside.
They wanted to see what
the fire was all about.
Oh, my! A pie was in the oven.
It had burned up.
What a mess!

So they cleaned up the mess.
Then Katie Kitty made
another pie.
And everyone sat down
and ate it.

Smokey's Day Off
From Work

It was Smokey's day off from work.
"I need some rest,"
he said to Katie Kitty.
"How about spending a quiet day
in the country with me?"
"That sounds very nice," said Katie.

So Smokey and Katie
went on a picnic.
Smokey brought sandwiches.
He brought milk.
Katie brought some blueberry pies.
What a good lunch they had!

Then they went to the pond.
They watched the frogs swimming.
It was very quiet.
Smokey almost fell asleep.

All at once they heard loud voices.
The voices said, "Help! Help!
Come quick!"

Smokey and Katie saw
Patrick and Penny Pig.
"Our barn is on fire!"
shouted Penny.
"We are here!" said Smokey.
"We will help!

"Are all your animals safe?"
asked Smokey.
"Yes," said Patrick.
Smokey had to think fast.
He did not have his fire engine.
He did not have his fire hose.
What could he do?

"Quick!" shouted Smokey.
"We must go to the well!"
At the well they met Farmer Fox.
He wanted to help, too.

Smokey told them all what to do.
Patrick got water in pails from the well.
He gave them to Penny.

Penny gave them to Katie.
Katie gave them to Smokey.
Smokey was up on a ladder.

Smokey threw water on the fire.

Farmer Fox was waiting.
Smokey threw down the empty pails to him.

Farmer Fox ran with the
empty pails to the well.
He gave the pails to Patrick.
Then Patrick filled them again.

Soon the fire was out.
"Thank you, Smokey!"
said Patrick and Penny.
"You saved our barn."

"Our day was not quiet,"
said Smokey. "But we all did
what I do best when I work.
We put the fire out!
Now we can rest—"
"And have some more pie!"
said Katie.
And they all ate lots of pie.